David Kirk's
NOVA
THE ROBOT

Twinkle Twinkle, Little Hedgehog

CALLAWAY & KIRK

NEW YORK

winkle the Hedgehog liked to snuggle. When Nova created Twinkle, he borrowed circuits from a spaceship's docking system, so nuzzling close to others was in Twinkle's wiring.

But there was a small problem— his spikes. They were long, needle sharp, and there were lots of them.

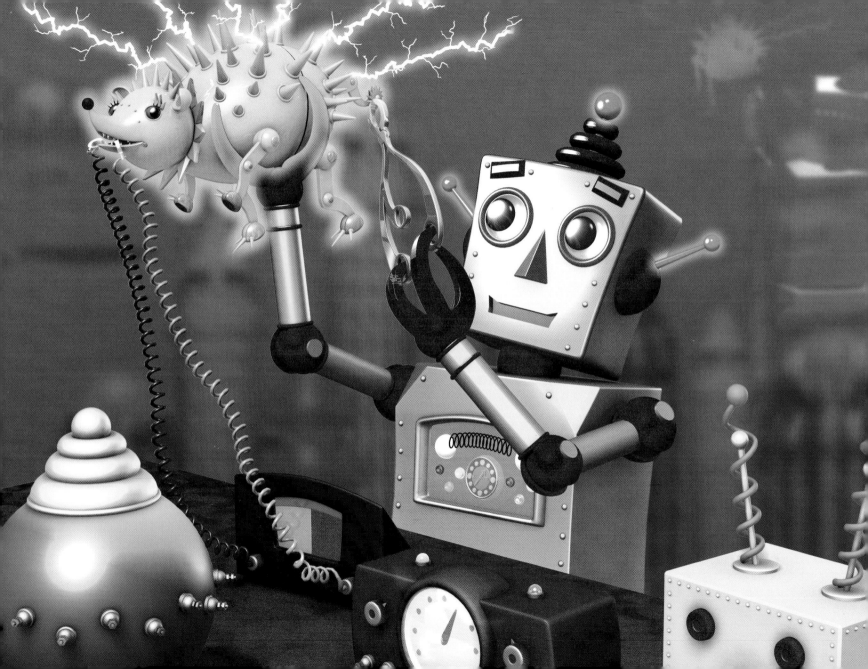

And that wasn't even the worst thing. When Nova built Twinkle, he figured that on a planet of metal robots, plain, old everyday spikes would hardly do. So, to make him all the hedgehog he could be, Nova charged his spikes with powerful electric shocks.

Poor hedgehog! Twinkle wanted to get close to everybody, but nobody wanted to get close to Twinkle.

He tried to curl up against Sparky #2 for a nice afternoon snooze, but instead, sent him whining into the closet.

He cozied up behind Cathode the Cat . . .

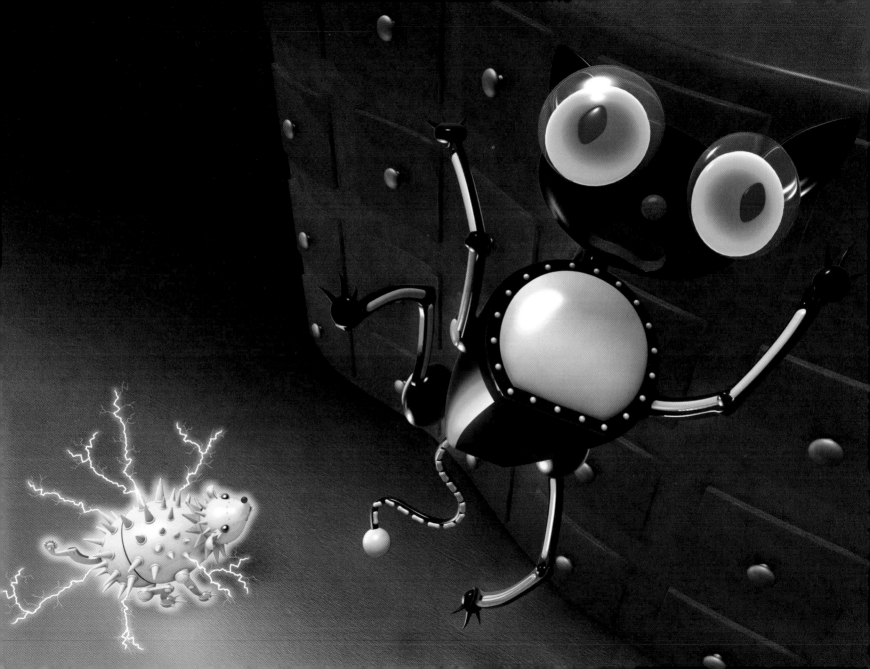

And launched her to the top of a cupboard.

Stuff the Turkey lost eleven tail feathers just brushing one of Twinkle's electric spikes with his toe.

And Nova's mother, Luna, didn't appreciate it in the least when he pinned himself to the inside of her skirt.

The harder Twinkle tried to be friendly, the more the other robots ran away.

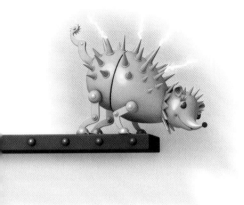

He took to laying in wait for his friends, dropping in on them when they least expected it. That was fine as far as it went. Still, nobody ever stayed around to cuddle.

The last straw was when he balled himself up in the bottom of Nova's dad, Taspett's boot.

winkle was put in a tiny cage. Now he had no hope of cuddling with anyone. He was miserable.

He wouldn't touch his oil broth. He wouldn't take a fresh charge for his batteries, which were terribly low. "If I have no charge," he thought, "I can't shock anyone. Maybe then they'll like me."

His batteries on zero, Twinkle fell into a deep sleep. Nova took the motionless hedgehog from his cage. There must be something he could do for poor Twinkle, but what?

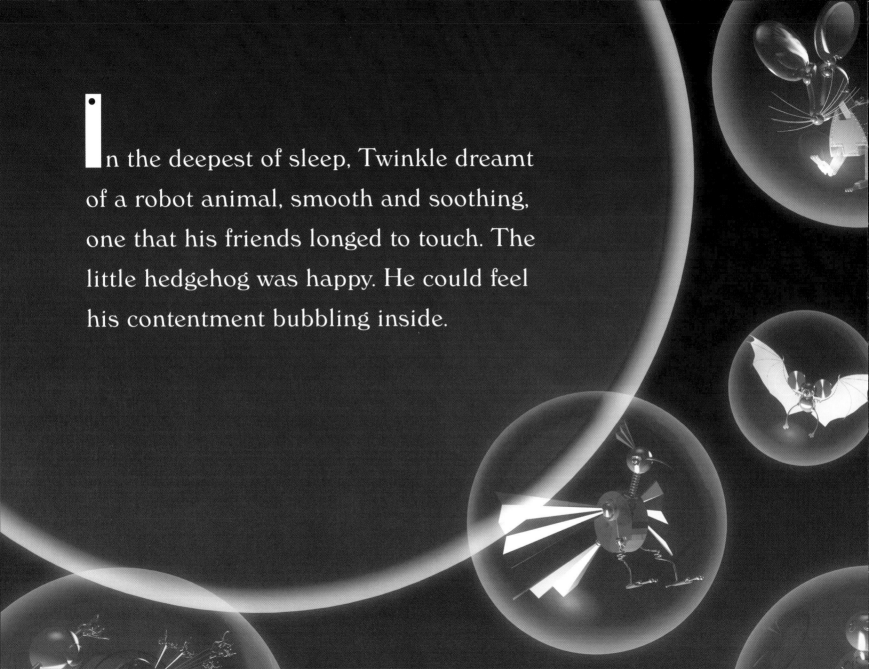

In the deepest of sleep, Twinkle dreamt of a robot animal, smooth and soothing, one that his friends longed to touch. The little hedgehog was happy. He could feel his contentment bubbling inside.

He woke from his dream with everyone gathered around. Cathode the Cat was nudging him with her nose. She didn't even jump when she touched him. Carefully clenching a spike between his teeth, Sparky lifted Twinkle gently into Nova's hands.

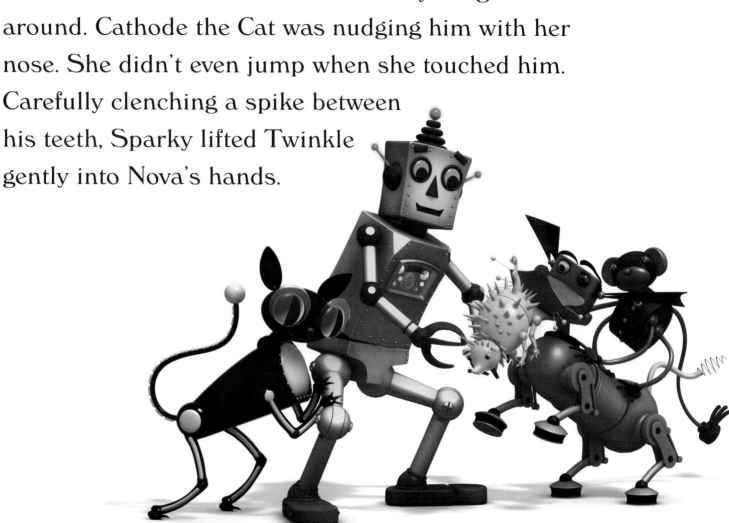

"**Y**ou still have a sting, Twinkle," Nova said, "but only when you want one. I gave you full control of your shock amplifier. Try it."

Nova set Twinkle down. Twinkle had only to think of electricity before bolts of energy sparked from spike to spike. Then he thought of his friends . . .

And the sparking stopped!

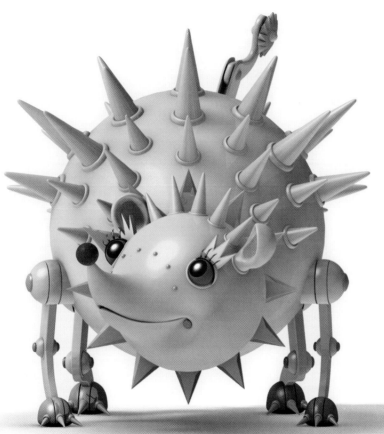

Twinkle never shocked anyone again . . .

Except once in a while accidentally, a few times when somebody was really asking for it . . .

or on very special occasions, just for fun.

For Primrose and Wisteria, who make the sparks fly.

Nicholas Callaway, President and Publisher
Antoinette White, Senior Editor · Toshiya Masuda, Art Director
George Gould, Production Director · Joya Rajadhyaksha, Associate Editor
Ivan Wong, Jr. and José Rodríguez, Production · Sofia Dumery, Design
Doug Vitarelli, Director of Animation · Raphael Shea, Art Assistant
Amy Cloud, Assistant Editor · Katy Leibold, Publishing Assistant · Krupa Jhaveri, Design Assistant
Kathryn Bradwell, Executive Assistant to the Publisher

David Kirk would also like to thank Bill Burg and Cara Paul.

Library of Congress Cataloging-in-Publication Data available upon request.

Distributed in the United States by Viking Children's Books.

Callaway Arts & Entertainment, the Callaway logotype, and Callaway & Kirk Company LLC are trademarks.

ISBN 0-448-43818-6

Visit Callaway at www.callaway.com

10 9 8 7 6 5 4 3 2 1   05 06 07 08 09 10

First edition, January 2005
Printed in Mexico